Giant-Sized Butterflies on My First Day of School

Justin Roberts   illustrated by Paola Escobar

G. P. Putnam's Sons

I feel so nervous in the morning light.

My mom says it'll be all right,

but I have giant-sized butterflies
on my first day.

So she makes me some hot oatmeal.
It doesn't change the way I feel.

How am I to know how it will go
on my first day?

We're in the car and we're on our way.

"When we get there, Mom, will you stay?
On my first day?"

Then Mom says, "When you first came—
when we met you—we felt the same.

"We had giant-sized butterflies
on our first day.

"And if there were some kind of magic spell that could protect like a turtle's shell, everyone would be wearing one on their first day."

Then Mom opens the back-seat door,

and tells me what butterflies are for—

"Don't hold them in,
just let them fly.

'Cause they were born to be your guide.

"Like monarchs helping flowers bloom,
our butterflies tell us we have room—

To learn from adventures
about to begin
on your first day.

"Those butterflies just help us grow.

It's a bit scary," Mom says. "I know!"

Now Mom's beside me and the school's in sight,
and everything is gonna be all right.

It's my first day,
and my butterflies are giant-sized.

It's my first day,
and those butterflies made me realize . . .

that the flutters inside
are wings opening wide . . .

guiding me through my first day.

For Mom. Thanks for guiding me
through so many first days.
—J.R.

For Mom, with love.
—P.E.

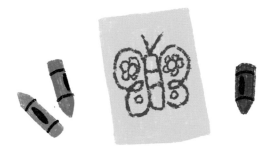

G. P. Putnam's Sons
An imprint of Penguin Random House LLC, New York

First published in the United States of America by G. P. Putnam's Sons,
an imprint of Penguin Random House LLC, 2023

Text copyright © 2023 by Justin Roberts
Illustrations copyright © 2023 by Paola Escobar

G. P. Putnam's Sons is a registered trademark of Penguin Random House LLC.
The Penguin colophon is a registered trademark of Penguin Books Limited.

Visit us online at penguinrandomhouse.com.

Library of Congress Cataloging-in-Publication Data
Names: Roberts, Justin, author. | Escobar, Paola, illustrator.
Title: Giant-sized butterflies on my first day of school / Justin Roberts; illustrated by Paola Escobar.
Description: New York: G. P. Putnam's Sons, 2023. | Summary: "On the first day of school, a girl learns how the giant butterflies in her stomach mean she's learning and growing"—Provided by publisher.
Identifiers: LCCN 2022006952 (print) | LCCN 2022006953 (ebook) | ISBN 9780525516439 (hardcover) | ISBN 9780525516460 (kindle edition) | ISBN 9780525516446 (epub)
Subjects: CYAC: First day of school—Fiction. | LCGFT: Picture Books.
Classification: LCC PZ7.R543244 Gi 2023 (print) | LCC PZ7.R543244 (ebook) | DDC [E]—dc23
LC record available at https://lccn.loc.gov/2022006952
LC ebook record available at https://lccn.loc.gov/2022006953

Manufactured in China

ISBN 9780525516439
1 3 5 7 9 10 8 6 4 2
TOPL

Design by Eileen Savage | Text set in Franziska Pro
This book was sketched and colored in Adobe Photoshop, using digital gouache brushes.